HOPE'S GIFT

Story and Pictures by Catherine Brighton

Doubleday
New York

y name is Mercy.
When I was ten our home was a row of
swaying wagons.

My family were actors. We were called the Van
Missen Traveling Delight Show.

I had a brother called Samson and a sister called
Hope.

We would be rocked to sleep by the rise and dip of
bumpy roads and woken in the dark by the cold
creeping under our blankets.

One sharp cold morning we came to a halt on the
grounds of a huge house.

As the wagons were unloaded in the dark, we three stood among the horses to keep warm. Peacocks were dragging their long tails across the lawn and screeching.

Adolpho, the tiny man, told us to go off and play. "But don't go anywhere near his lordship's house or he'll be after you."

So we ran away, through the towering gates, away from the house, and down the road to the town.

We peeped in at the dark shopfronts and made silly faces at the butcher's boy.

A lady with black teeth gave us each a pie and we sat on a wall and swung our legs.

Hope was last to finish her pie. She always finished last, whether it was eating or dressing or anything else.

Sometimes, when we were in the play, she would forget her lines.

"It's easy," we would say, and laugh at her.

Adolpho said she was special.

But she was so slow that she never knew we were teasing her.

She did know how to make friends, though.

While we were exploring the narrow streets Hope met a boy called Joachim.

He took us to his house, down an alley.

In his yard there were caged birds singing, and among the singing there was a funny voice that kept repeating:

"Have hope, have mercy."

"That's our talking parakeet," said Joachim, putting out a finger.

"I like him," said Hope, and the parakeet hopped on to her head.

"He can't fly," Joachim explained. "He was born with a dragging wing."

Then something very strange happened.

ope took the bird from her head with both hands.

She held it gently-firm until it was still.

When she opened her hands the parakeet fluttered free and flew on to the roof.

"How did you do that?" asked Joachim.

"She mended its wing," I whispered in awe.

But then Joachim's mother called, so we went back onto the street.

In the garden of the big house, the first performance was just starting.

A very royal-looking boy stood behind a girl in an invalid chair. Her legs were covered by a rug.

"Why is she sitting like that?" I asked.

"My sister cannot walk," said the boy. "She never will."

He turned away to watch the show.

ell" — I started again — "you may be glad you met me."

"I doubt it," he said, looking down his nose.

"My sister Hope, she can make sick birds better. She could do it for your sister. She only charges one gold sovereign."

He hesitated, and I kept on arguing.

"Very well," he said at last. "Angelica and I will receive you in the nursery wing this afternoon. You had better be right. If there is one thing I cannot stand, it is grasping poor people who will do anything for money."

ater in the afternoon the stage was covered by a bright curtain and flags fluttered gently from the poles.

Our family was resting in the wagons.

"Follow me," I said to Hope and Samson.

As we made our way through the garden, I explained about Angelica's legs.

"But we mustn't go near the house. Adolpho warned us not to," said Samson.

"Oh, Mercy, supposing we get caught, supposing I can't mend her legs," moaned Hope.

nside, the house was as big as a church. Angelica's bed had a roof.

As I passed her brother I whispered, "Let's see the money then."

He opened his hand to show the coin.

Hope approached Angelica's bed and I glanced across at Samson, who shrugged. He didn't believe that Hope could do it and I wasn't too sure either.

e seemed to wait forever. The room was silent. Hope's tears plopped onto the coverlet.

"She can't do it. I knew she was a fake," said the boy. "I am going to get my father. He will lock you up." And he strode out of the room.

"Come on. Let's get out of here before we're caught," I called to Samson.

"No. Look, Mercy. Look."

e turned to where Hope was standing by the bed.

Her hands were resting on Angelica's legs. They were *moving*.

Very slowly Angelica slid her legs to the floor. We panicked and ran for the door.

We scrambled down the stairs, and as I reached the landing I turned and saw Angelica standing.

She was saying, "Thank you, Hope."

Hope didn't hear, nor did Samson, for already they were tearing across the lawn in the evening gloom.

We hid in the costume wagon.
All night we lay there, covered by velvet costumes. We could hear the sounds of the show and see the lights of the stage. We were frightened of what we had done and frightened of his lordship coming to get us.

No one came looking.

We woke next morning before light.

The Van Missens packed up the show in the dark. Very quietly the wagon rumbled through the gates.

Dawn was breaking as we passed through the town. Suddenly we heard a voice shouting, "Stop! Wait!" I was cold with fear.

ut it was Joachim.
He was running by the wagons with the parakeet on his arm.

"Hope," he called. "Please take the bird. I want you to have it."

The parakeet rose, circled, and flew onto Hope's outstretched hand.

"Well," I said. "It's your very own bird."

"It's a gift," said Samson.

"It's my gift," said Hope. "Thank you, Joachim, and . . . goodbye."

Joachim waved as our wagon left town.

For Phyllis

LIBRARY OF CONGRESS
Library of Congress Cataloging-in-Publication Data

Brighton, Catherine.
Hope's gift : story and pictures / by Catherine Brighton.
p.   cm.
Summary: Hope, considered to be the "slow one" of three children in
a family of traveling actors in sixteenth-century Europe, discovers
that she has a gift for healing the sick — a gift that is not for sale,
despite her sister's plans.
ISBN 0-385-24598-X   ISBN 0-385-24599-8 (lib. bdg.)
[1. Healers — Fiction. 2. Sisters — Fiction.] I. Title.
PZ7.B76524Ho 1988
[E] — dc19